VOL. 12

Story by HIDENORI KUSAKA
Art by SATOSHI YAMAMOTO

Pokémon Black and White
Volume 12
VIZ Kids Edition

Story by HIDENORI KUSAKA
Art by SATOSHI YAMAMOTO

English Adaptation / Bryant Turnage
Translation / Tetsuichiro Miyaki
Touch-up & Lettering / Susan Daigle-Leach
Cover Art Assist / Kaillash Black, Walden Wong
Design / Fawn Lau
Editor / Annette Roman

Printed in the U.S.A.

Published by VIZ Media, LLC
P.O. Box 77010
San Francisco, CA 94107

10 9 8 7 6 5 4 3 2 1
First printing, October 2013

BLACK AND WHITE

VOL.12

THE STORY THUS FAR!

Pokémon Trainer Black is exploring the mysterious Unova region with his brand-new Pokédex. Pokémon Trainer White runs a thriving talent agency for performing Pokémon. While traveling together, their paths cross with Team Plasma, a nefarious group that advocates releasing your Pokémon into the wild! Now Black and White are off on their own separate journeys of discovery...

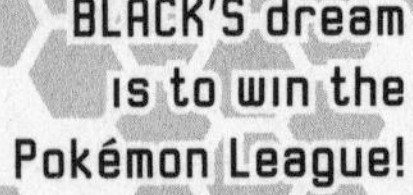

BLACK'S dream is to win the Pokémon League!

WHITE'S dream is to make her Tepig Gigi a star!

Black's Munna, MUSHA, helps him think clearly by temporarily "eating" his dream.

White's Tepig, GIGI, and Black's Emboar, BO, get along like peanut butter and jelly! But now Gigi has left White for another Trainer...

Adventure 38
Decisions, Decisions...

rmbl rmbl rmbl rmbl rmbl rmbl

rmbl rmbl rmbl rmbl rmbl

vroooa
WHOA!!
HUH?

WHERE AM I ...?!
rtt/ rtt/

rmmmb

THE TUBE-LINE BRIDGE.

THE BRIDGE THE BATTLE SUBWAY RUNS THROUGH.

WE'RE ON TOP OF IT.

OH! IT'S ALL COMING BACK TO ME NOW...

TEAM PLASMA TRICKED ME WITH AN IMPOSTER OF YOU! AND, AND...

...GHET-SIS...
...STOLE THE DARK STONE!!

AS I'M SURE YOU KNOW...
...ALL THE GYM LEADERS WHO WERE PRESENT DURING THE ROBBERY HAVE BEEN KIDNAPPED—APART FROM ME.

WE WERE GOING TO LAUNCH A DIRECT ASSAULT ON THE ENEMY HEADQUARTERS TO BRING AN END TO ALL THIS...
BUT THE ODDS ARE AGAINST US NOW.

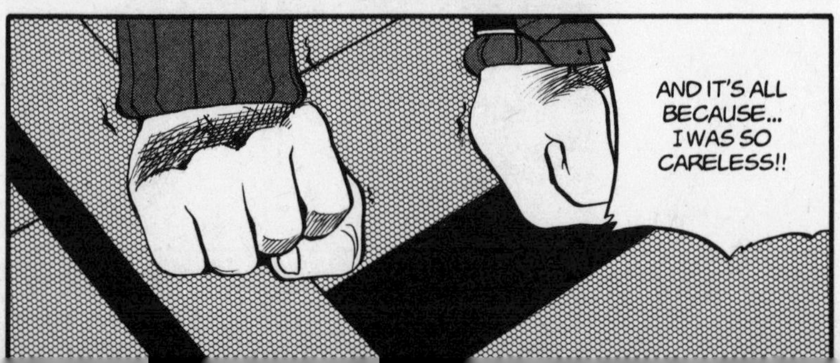
AND IT'S ALL BECAUSE... I WAS SO CARELESS!!

HUH?

WHAT IS THIS, BRYCEN?!

ISN'T IT OBVIOUS? IT'S CRYO-GONAL'S ICE CHAIN.

I DON'T WANT YOU TO...

...RUN AWAY.

IT'S PART OF YOUR TRAINING TODAY.

NO.
RUN AWAY? IS THIS SOME KIND OF JOKE?!

TRAINING ...?

ARE YOU STRONG ENOUGH TO DEFEAT AN ENEMY...
...WITH THE POWER TO CAP-TURE ALL THOSE GYM LEADERS IN ONE FELL SWOOP?

DO YOU KNOW WHERE TEAM PLASMA'S SO-CALLED CASTLE IS LOCATED?

LET'S SEE IF YOU CAN BREAK FREE OF THAT ICE CHAIN FIRST.
IF YOU CAN'T EVEN DO THAT—THERE'S NO POINT IN ATTEMPTING ANY DRAMATIC RESCUE MISSIONS.
OKAY, FINE! I'LL SHOW YOU WHAT I'VE GOT!!
toss
BOOM
I'LL BURN THROUGH THIS ICE CHAIN WITH A FIRE-TYPE MOVE!!
DO IT!!

THEN I'LL CALL YOU... UM...

EM-BOAR, HUH...?

•006 Emboar
Mega Fire Pig Pokémon
HT 5'03"
WT 330.7 lbs.
It can throw a fire punch by setting its fists on fire with its fiery chin. It cares deeply about its friends.
INFO AREA CRY FORMS

HMM. SINCE YOU'VE EVOLVED, I OUGHT TO GIVE YOU A NEW NICKNAME.

...NITE.

IT'S NO USE. YOU'LL ROAST MY LEG BEFORE YOU MELT THE CHAIN...

hff hff

...BO...

...FROM NOW ON!

GOOD NAME.

YOU SHOULD TRAIN IT...

...TO BE A MARTIAL ARTS KING.

YOU'VE GOT OTHERS WITH YOU...?

I'LL COME UP WITH A DIFFERENT TRAINING REGIMEN FOR YOUR MUNNA, GALVANTULA AND TIRTOUGA.

BRING THEM OUT.

GOOD JOB, BRYCEN!

I'M NOT SURE ABOUT THAT... AM I DOING THE RIGHT THING?
WHAT ARE YOU WOR-RIED ABOUT?
JUST AS THE DARK STONE IS ZEKROM...
...THE LIGHT STONE IS RESHI-RAM.
THE OTHER STONE... THE LIGHT STONE...
...ROLLED OVER TO THAT KID, RIGHT?
THERE'S A POSSI-BILITY...
...THAT HE WAS ***CHOSEN***...
...TO BE THE ***HERO***.
IT'S NO ORDI-NARY STONE, AFTER ALL.
THAT LEGENDARY POKÉMON ***CHOSE*** THAT BOY.
IT WOULDN'T HURT TO PREPARE OURSELVES WITH THAT POSSIBILITY IN MIND.

WITHOUT THE OTHER GYM LEADERS TO COUNT ON, I HAVE HIGH EXPECTATIONS FOR THAT BOY—HE'S EARNED SIX GYM BADGES ALREADY.
THAT'S WHY I BROUGHT HIM HERE IN THE FIRST PLACE.
I AGREE THAT YOU SHOULD TRAIN HIM.
...

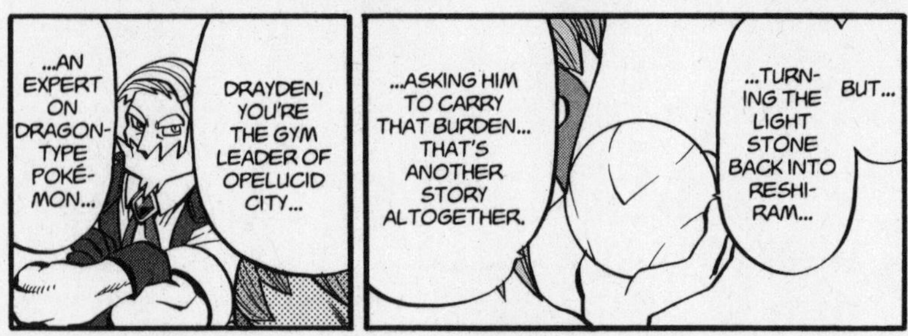
DRAYDEN, YOU'RE THE GYM LEADER OF OPELUCID CITY...
...AN EXPERT ON DRAGON-TYPE POKÉMON...
BUT...
...TURNING THE LIGHT STONE BACK INTO RESHIRAM...
...ASKING HIM TO CARRY THAT BURDEN... THAT'S ANOTHER STORY ALTOGETHER.

CLAY DUG UP THE LIGHT STONE AND THE DARK STONE ***TOGETHER***.
WHEN LENORA HEARD ABOUT IT, SHE IMMEDIATELY RECALLED THE LEGEND OF UNOVA...
...AND PURPOSEFULLY SPREAD THE NEWS ABOUT THE DARK STONE'S DISCOVERY... USING ALL THE MEDIA ATTENTION TO HIDE THE FACT THAT THE LIGHT STONE HAD BEEN SECRETLY BROUGHT TO HER MUSEUM.
AFTER THAT, SHE ASKED YOU TO FIND OUT MORE ABOUT THE TWO STONES.

I'VE HEARD THAT BOTH ZEKROM AND RESHIRAM TRANS-FORMED INTO THESE STONES OF THEIR OWN FREE WILL.

SEALING THEMSELVES IN BODIES OF STONE FOR SOME REASON...

IS FORCING THAT SEAL OPEN AGAIN REALLY THE RIGHT THING TO DO?!

rmbl
rmbl
rmbl
rmbl

YOU BOTH HAVE TO CALM DOWN...
...AND GET ALONG WITH EACH OTHER.

THIS IS IRIS.
SHE'S TRAINING UNDER ME TO BECOME A DRAGON-TYPE POKÉMON EXPERT.
PERSONALLY, I THINK SHE'S AS SKILLED AS THAT BOY.
THAT'S WHY I BROUGHT HER WITH ME.

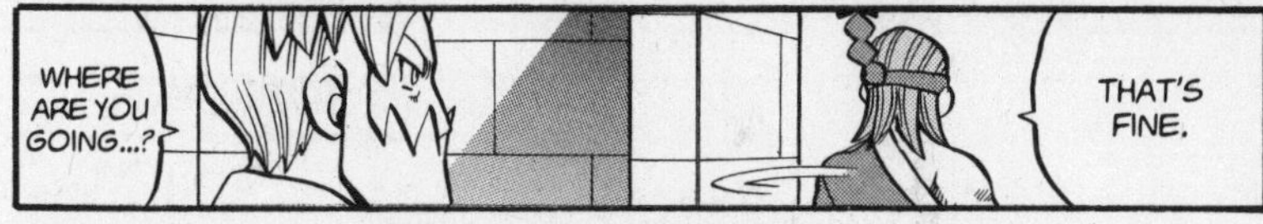
THAT'S FINE.
WHERE ARE YOU GOING...?

TO FIND THE HEADQUARTERS OF TEAM PLASMA—THEIR CASTLE.
I HAVE TO FIGURE OUT WHERE IT'S LOCATED.

OKAY, BO!

THE ICE CHAIN IS CRE-ATED BY...
...CRYO-GONAL!

AS SOON AS WE DEFEAT CRYO-GONAL...
rmbl
rmbl
rmbl
rmbl
...WE'LL BE FREE OF THIS CHAIN!!

rmbl
FLAME-THROWER!!
rmbl
rmbl
rmbl

KWAFOOSH
OWW-WWW!!

NUTS! THE TRAIN KEEPS ARRIVING AND MESSING UP OUR AIM JUST AS WE'RE ABOUT TO ATTACK!
RMBL
TRY AGAIN! NOW'S OUR CHANCE!!
FOOSH
FSSSS

IT... DISAP-PEARED?!
NO... WAIT!
•121 Cryogonal
Crystallizing Pokémon
HT 3'07"
WT 326.3 lbs.
When its body temperature goes up, it turns into steam and vanishes. When its temperature lowers, it returns to ice.
INFO AREA CRY FORMS
BO'S FIRE TURNED ITS BODY INTO STEAM... AND NOW IT'S GONE!

WOM
HOW CAN WE FIGHT IF...
...WE CAN'T EVEN SEE OUR OPPO-NENT ?!

STOP! IT'S ONLY GOING TO MAKE THINGS HARDER FOR US IF YOU BREATHE FIRE ON IT!

IT'S NO USE! TEP HATED TO LOSE...
NITE WAS RECK-LESS...
AND BO IS LIKE BOTH OF THEM PUT TOGETHER— AS A MATTER OF FACT, BO IS WORSE!

WOM...

FSSS...

AAH!! THERE IT IS!

LISTEN TO ME, BO! IT WON'T DO ANY GOOD TO ATTACK IT WITH FIRE.

SMASH

MARTIAL ARTS... FIGHTING...

WE'RE NOT SUPPOSED TO BE USING FIRE-TYPE MOVES! WE'RE SUPPOSED TO USE ***FIGHTING-TYPE*** MOVES!

BO, DO IT AGAIN!!

HAMMER ARM!!

ting
THE CRYOGONAL IS SO COLD IT FREEZES BO'S ARM WHEN BO PUNCHES IT!
BO'S ARM...
OH...!
GREAT!
tff tff tff tff
THIS IS...
...OUR GOAL!
BO SEEMS TO BE TAKING THIS FIGHT PRETTY SERIOUSLY.
OUR PRIMARY GOAL ISN'T TO HAVE A POKÉMON BATTLE RIGHT NOW!
HOLD IT, BO!

THIS CHAIN AROUND MY LEG...
YOU HAVE TO SMASH IT WITH YOUR FIST!
BUT... BE CAREFUL NOT TO SMASH MY LEG ALONG WITH IT.

TO TOP IT OFF...

...YOU HAVE TO DO IT ON TOP OF THIS BRIDGE THAT...
...SHAKES EVERY TIME A TRAIN PASSES BY!!

CAN YOU DO IT, BO...?

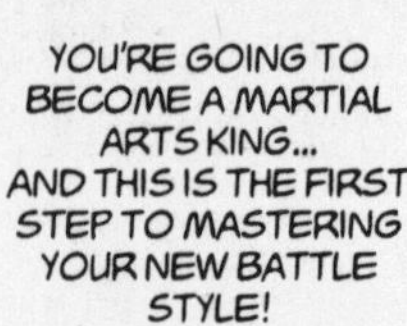
YOU'RE GOING TO BECOME A MARTIAL ARTS KING... AND THIS IS THE FIRST STEP TO MASTERING YOUR NEW BATTLE STYLE!

I TRUST YOU. I KNOW YOU'VE GOT WHAT IT TAKES.
WE'VE COME THIS FAR TOGETHER.
YOU CAN DO IT WITH YOUR POWER AND PRECISION!
GO FOR IT!

I WANT YOU...
...TO TRUST ME TOO.

vroar
vrroar

rmbl
rmbl
rmbl

rmbl rmbl

SSh

krick
shattr

YOU DID IT...
...BO!

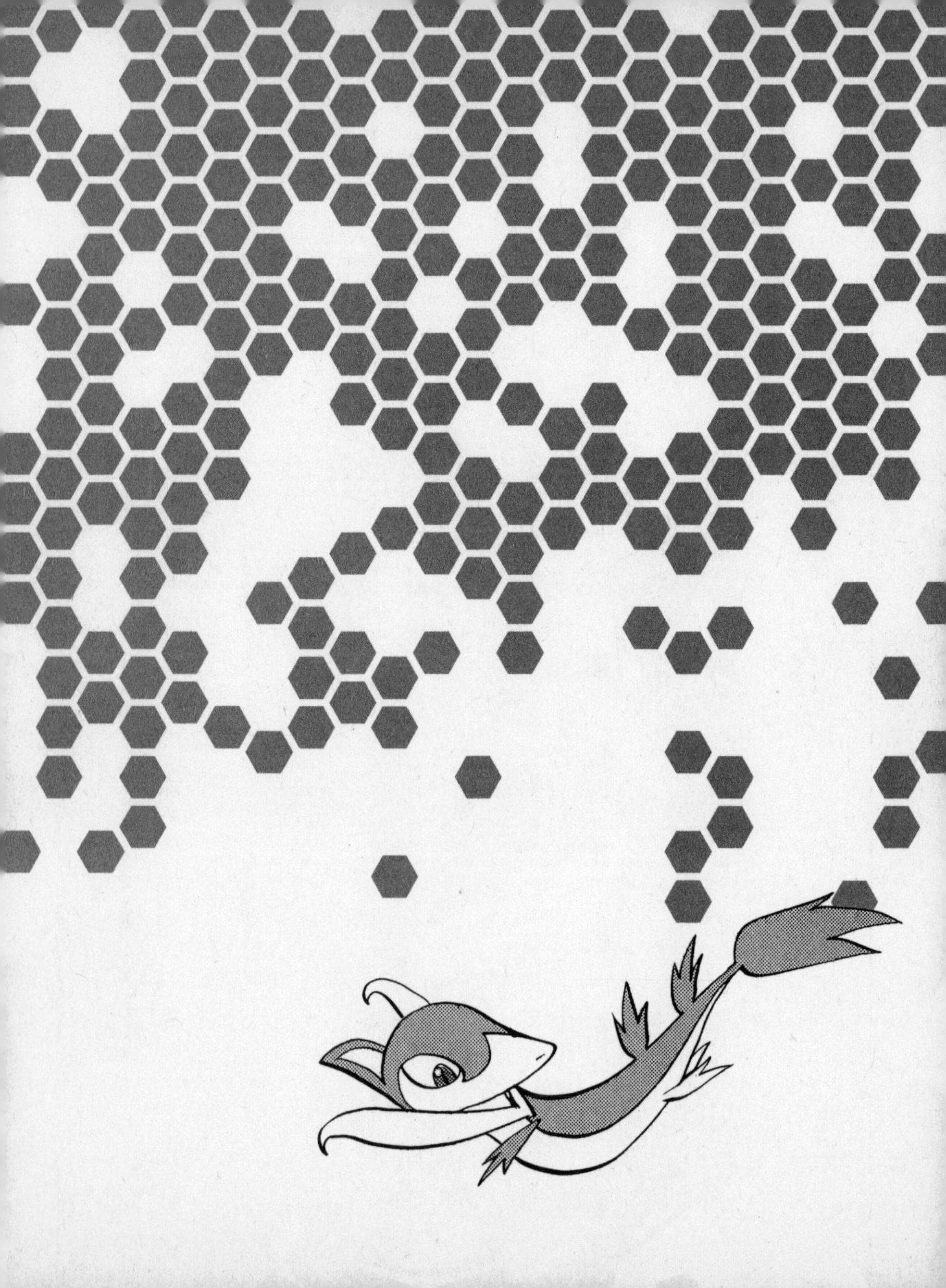

Adventure 39
School of Hard Knocks

DRAGON-SPIRAL TOWER...
ACCORDING TO DRAYDEN'S INVESTIGATION...
...THIS IS THE PLACE FOR THOSE WHO WANT TO LEARN ABOUT THE LEGENDARY DRAGON-TYPE POKÉMON.
BUT IT'S NOTHING BUT A HUGE MAZE TO ME...
HOW AM I SUPPOSED TO FIND ANYTHING HERE?!

SO THIS IS WHERE YOU RECLAIMED YOUR FORM...

...ZEK-ROM!

WHERE IS TEAM PLASMA'S HEAD-QUARTERS? THIS PLACE THEY CALL THEIR CASTLE...
WE'RE HEADING FOR THE CASTLE.
WHERE ARE YOU NOW...?
AND WHAT OF THE GYM LEAD-ERS...?
I CAN'T FIND ANY OTHER TRACE OF THEM...

RUINS, CAVES, ABANDONED HOUSES, BUILDINGS UNDER CONSTRUCTION... I'VE SEARCHED STRUCTURES WHERE LARGE NUMBERS OF PEOPLE COULD EASILY COME AND GO...
BUT I HAVEN'T FOUND HIDE NOR HAIR OF THEM...

NOT A SIGN OF CLAY, LENORA, ELESA, SKYLA, BURGH...
WHERE **ARE** YOU?!

TUBE-LINE BRIDGE ...

tink tink tink ...

YOU DID IT, BO!
WE MADE IT THROUGH BRYCEN'S TRAINING SESSION!!
OWWWW!! AND NOW THE PAIN SETS IN...!
OH, DEAR.
I'LL TEND TO YOUR WOUNDS RIGHT AWAY!
THANKS, DOC-TOR... UM...
...LOGAN.
DOCTOR LOGAN.
IMPRES-SIVE!
clap clap clap
YOU MANAGED TO SHATTER CRYO-GONAL'S ICE CHAIN!
AND *YOU* ARE ...?!

THE MAYOR AND GYM LEADER OF OPELUCID CITY...
...DRAYDEN!

THAT'S WHY I SENT IRIS TO CASTELIA CITY.
THEY WERE HOLDING A "LEGENDS OF UNOVA REGION EXHIBITION," WHICH INCLUDED A NUMBER OF EXHIBITS ABOUT DRAGON-TYPE POKÉMON.

DRUD-DIGON...
BOOM

creep
creep
gulp
SMACK
DRAGON TAIL!
GO!!

pat
pat

yoink

kwafoom!
AND THERE YOU HAVE IT.

NICE WORK, DRUD-DIGON.

shvvr

THAT DRUDDIGON GIVES OFF SUCH AN INTENSE VIBE...
BO FELT IT TOO.

IF I'M GOING TO COLLECT ALL MY BADGES TO ENTER THE POKÉMON LEAGUE...
...I'LL HAVE TO FACE THIS GYM LEADER!
catch

BUT THE WAY THINGS ARE GOING...
...WILL THEY EVEN HOLD THE POKÉMON LEAGUE THIS YEAR?!

BLACK...
HUH?

YOU MANAGED TO ESCAPE FROM THE ICE CHAIN...

...THAT BRYCEN SET AS YOUR GOAL.

AND YOUR TIRTOUGA, MUNNA AND GALVANTULA ALL SUCCEEDED IN DEFEATING THE VANILLISH.
THIS ENDS YOUR TRAINING SESSION AT THE TUBELINE BRIDGE.

WE HAVE TO MOVE ON TO YOUR NEXT SESSION. C'MON, LET'S GO!
N-NEXT SESSION...?

BLACK, TAKE IRIS WITH YOU. I'M SURE SHE'LL LEARN A LOT FROM YOUR TRAINING AS WELL.
WHAT?!
THANKS!

AND, BLACK...

I'M COUNTING ON YOU.
I WANT YOU TO BECOME THE "TRUTH" TO FIGHT AGAINST THE "IDEAL"!
grip
...
SO... WHAT'S NEXT?
UM, ACCORDING TO THE ORDERS I RECEIVED FROM BRYCEN...
Vrrmmmmbl

A...
BIKER
GANG
?!
COME ON,
COME ON!
LET'S GO,
BLACK!
BUT...
HOW ARE
WE GOING
TO...?
HEY!

HEY, KID!!!
YOU WANNA CROSS THIS BRIDGE?

YES.
OH YEAH? WHO GAVE YOU PERMIS-SION?

SINCE WHEN DO I NEED PERMIS-SION?!
AND WHO WOULD I ASK, ANY-WAY?

VROOM
ME! YOU ASK FOR *MY* PERMIS-SION!!
VROOM
THE NAME'S JEREMY—LEADER OF THE BLACK EMPOLEON BIKER GANG!!
VROOM

LET'S GO ANOTHER WAY, LOGAN. NO POINT WASTING TIME ON THESE LOSERS.
YOU CAN'T DO THAT.
WHY NOT?
BECAUSE *THIS* IS YOUR NEXT **TRAINING SESSION.**

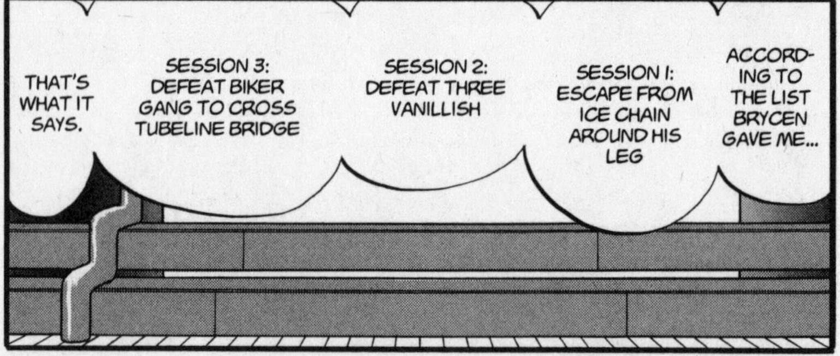

ACCORDING TO THE LIST BRYCEN GAVE ME...
SESSION 1: ESCAPE FROM ICE CHAIN AROUND HIS LEG
SESSION 2: DEFEAT THREE VANILLISH
SESSION 3: DEFEAT BIKER GANG TO CROSS TUBELINE BRIDGE
THAT'S WHAT IT SAYS.

NO WAY...
HEY!!
YOU WANNA PIECE OF US?!
BRING IT ON!!

THAT KID THINKS HE'S GONNA BEAT US?! HA!
EVER SINCE OUR SECOND-IN-COMMAND LEFT, EVERY-ONE AND HIS GRANDMA WANTS TO CHALLENGE US!
SIGH... OUR SECOND-IN-COMMAND AND HIS DUCKLETT WERE AN INVINCIBLE PAIR.
WHAT'S HE DOING NOW...?
I HEARD HE LET GO OF HIS DUCKLETT AND... PSST, PSST...
WHOA, SERI-OUSLY?!

WILL YOU GUYS SHUT IT!!
IT'S TIME TA SHOW THIS KID HOW TOUGH WE ARE!
YEAH!!

THE TUBELINE BRIDGE AT NIGHT IS THE LAST STOMPING GROUND FOR BLACK EMPOLEON!
VROOM
SQUASH THAT KID FLAT!!

YEAAAAH!!
YEE-HAW!!

HUH?
WHAT?
YIKES!
yoink
yoink
yoink

WHAT THE...?!

Krash

fwump

AAAARGH!!

TULA TRIPPED UP MORE THAN A DOZEN BIKES CHARGING TOWARDS ME AT TOP SPEED AND PULLED THEM UP OFF THE GROUND...
snip
TULA HAS GOTTEN STRONG!

AIYEEE!!
krash smash
thunk
AAAARGH!!

WAA-ARGH!! MY MA-CHINE!!
I HAVEN'T FINISHED PAYING OFF MY LOAN ON IT!!
MY MOM BOUGHT IT FOR ME... SHE'S GONNA BE SO MAD!

YOU LITTLE BRAT!!

I'LL SHOW YOU HOW TOUGH...
...THE LEADER OF THIS GANG IS!!

I'M...
...OUT OF GAS?!
E
F

HUH?

chrrk chrrk

I FILLED THIS BABY UP WITH DELUXE HIGH OCTANE ON THE WAY HERE!!
THERE'S NO WAY IT COULD BE EMPTY!!

EVER HEAR OF A MOVE CALLED TELE-PORT?

MY MUSHA TELEPORTED THE GAS FROM YOUR BIKE INTO YOUR LEATHER PANTS.
AAAH!! I SHOULD HAVE GONE WITH UNLEADED GAS!!
splish splash
SIC 'IM, SCRAGGY!!
fwip fwip

COSTA! HYDRO PUMP!!
foosh
voing...
dodge
WHAT THE ...?!
THAT STREAM OF WATER JUST... CHANGED DIRECTION ?!

SPLASH SPLASH

WHOA, WHOA, WHOA!

DON'T COME NEAR ME!!

AND FROM THIS DAY ON, I'M CHANGING THE NAME OF OUR GANG TO ***BLACK TIRTOUGA***!

I WON'T TROUBLE YOU AGAIN!

Adventure 40
With a Little Help from My Friends

ANVILLE TOWN! ANVILLE TOWN!

FINAL STOP—ANVILLE TOWN!

THE FINAL STOP... FEELS LIKE I'VE BEEN RIDING THIS TRAIN ***FOREVER***!

BOOM
YOU DO REALIZE YOU'RE STILL IN THE MIDDLE OF YOUR FINAL BATTLE...
YOU'RE GOING TO LOSE AGAIN IF YOU LET YOUR GUARD DOWN.
WSHH WSH WSH WSH WSH
RIGHT !!
I'VE FINALLY BECOME GOOD ENOUGH TO COMPETE AGAINST THE SUBWAY BOSSES.
LET'S WIN THIS BATTLE AND PROVE HOW STRONG WE'VE GROWN!
LEAF STORM !!
HWOOOSH

HM...
hwoof

WHERE EXACTLY ARE YOU AIMING ...?
THIS IS WHERE YOU SHOULD AIM.
AT THE CORE OF MY KLINK-LANG.

YOU MUST BE RUTH-LESS IN BATTLE!

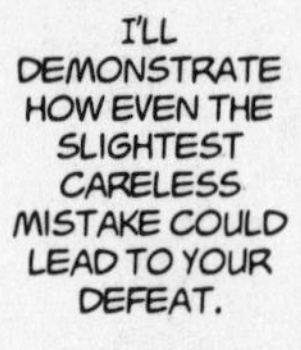
I'LL DEMONSTRATE HOW EVEN THE SLIGHTEST CARELESS MISTAKE COULD LEAD TO YOUR DEFEAT.

TURN YOUR GEARS !!
CHARGE UP YOUR ENERGY AND USE...

WHAT ?!

WHY WON'T YOU TURN?!

?
rnk rnk rnk

rnk rnk rnk rnk

LOOK, INGO! THE LEAVES FROM LEAF STORM ARE JAMMING THE GEAR WHEELS.
WHAT ?!
NOW!!

SLASH

A DRAW.
WE HAVE A DRAW!
WUMP

I CAN'T BELIEVE I FELL FOR SUCH A SIMPLE TRICK!
HEY, INGO... DID YOU KNOW THAT EVEN THE SLIGHTEST CARELESS MISTAKE COULD LEAD TO YOUR DEFEAT? HMM...?
RRGH ...

WHITE, THAT WAS SPLENDID. I'M IMPRESSED THAT YOU MANAGED TO COME AWAY WITH A DRAW.
HUR-RAY !!

WHY DON'T YOU HEAL YOUR POKÉMON, THEN TAKE A WELL-DESERVED BREAK? DO A LITTLE SIGHT-SEEING!
THIS TRAIN IS RETURNING TO NIMBASA CITY, BUT YOU STILL HAVE SOME TIME BEFORE IT DEPARTS.
GREAT IDEA! COME ON OUT, EVERY-BODY!
I'LL ADMIT, I HAD DOUBTS ABOUT YOU AT THE BEGINNING, BUT... YOU'VE FINALLY MANAGED TO PUT ON A DECENT POKÉMON BATTLE!
YOU'RE BEING TOO HARSH, EMMET.

THE NEW POKÉMON YOU CAPTURED ON THE WAY HERE ARE LOOKING GOOD TOO.
HEY...
HAVE YOU GIVEN THEM NICKNAMES YET?
OF COURSE!

DOROTHY.

NANCY.

SALLY.

AND THEN...
...THERE'S *THIS* POKÉMON...

...WHO'S BEEN FOLLOWING ME AROUND FOR SOME REASON...
I COULDN'T TELL IF IT WAS A FRIEND OR FOE AT FIRST...
BUT I'VE GOTTEN KIND OF ATTACHED TO IT SINCE WE'VE BEEN TRAINING TOGETHER...

MAYBE POKÉMON BATTLES...
...STRENGTHEN THE BONDS BETWEEN PEOPLE AND THEIR POKÉMON?

HERE. I WANT YOU TO COME WITH ME TOO...

...AMANDA.

tmp
MAYBE I'M TOO OPTI-MISTIC?

OUCH !!
smak

EH?
WHERE ARE YOU GOING ?!

!

THE SOUND OF... A FLUTE...
HOW PRETTY...
IT'S SO... UPLIFTING...
I WONDER IF THE POKÉMON ARE ATTRACTED TO THE MUSIC TOO!
THAT WOULDN'T SURPRISE ME. ***ANYONE*** WOULD WANT TO LISTEN TO SUCH BEAUTIFUL PLAYING...
OVER THERE...
OH! THAT'S...

HELLO
?
...UM...

YOU'RE... I KNOW YOU! WE MET IN STRIATON CITY AND CASTELIA CITY!
BIANCA!
YOU'RE BLACK'S CHILDHOOD FRIEND!
OH! HI, BOSS!!

IT'S A MUSICAL SCORE I WAS GIVEN AT THE TOWN GATE.
IT'S A LULLABY FOR THE TRAINS THAT SLEEP IN THIS TOWN.
I WISH I COULD PLAY AN INSTRU-MENT.
MY PARENTS HAD ME TAKE ALL SORTS OF LESSONS... PIANO, GUITAR AND WHATNOT. BUT I NEVER MASTERED ANY OF THEM.
LONG TIME NO SEE, WHITE!
SURE.
OH, PLEASE DON'T CALL ME BOSS! MY NAME'S WHITE. CALL ME WHITE.
OH, THAT TUNE I WAS PLAY-ING...?
WHAT A COINCIDENCE. THAT MELODY WAS SO BEAUTIFUL! SO SOOTHING...
WE HAVE TO GET A SNAP-SHOT OF IT!!
A RARE TRAIN CARRIAGE JUST ENTERED THE STATION !!
trmp! trmp!
TEE HEE! WELL, IF YOU ENJOYED THAT TUNE, I'LL PLAY IT AGAIN FOR YOU.
LOOK OUT ...!!
fwip
fwip
AIYEEE !!
fwip
fwip
OH... EEK...
AIIEEE! BIANCA!!

BUT I DO ENVY THEM...
YOU DO? WHY...?

ARE YOU ALL RIGHT?
HMPH. THOSE TRAIN FANS ARE SO ILL-MANNERED!
DON'T WORRY, I'M FINE.

I ENVY THEIR PASSION!
THEY'RE SO ENTHUSIASTIC ABOUT GETTING A PICTURE OF THAT SPECIAL TRAIN.

REALLY ENTHUSI-ASTIC...
THERE ISN'T ANYTHING I CAN THINK OF THAT I'M THAT ENTHUSIASTIC ABOUT...
SO I ENVY THEM...
HM...

I'M OVERHEARING AN INTERESTING DISCUSSION OVER HERE. IT SOUNDS PROFOUND, SO I'M GOING TO STAND NEARBY AND LISTEN IN. OH, DON'T LET ME DISTRACT YOU. GO AHEAD. KEEP TALKING.

WELL ...
WHAT IS *YOUR* DREAM, WHITE?
I'M TAKING A BREAK FROM IT RIGHT NOW... BUT IT'S DEFINITELY BEING INVOLVED IN SHOW BUSINESS. I HAVE NO DOUBTS ABOUT THAT.

REALLY ENTHUSIASTIC, HUH...?
THAT REMINDS ME OF BLACK...
YOU MUST HAVE HEARD HIM SHOUTING OUT HIS VOW TO WIN THE POKÉMON CHAMPIONSHIP ALL THE TIME, RIGHT?
YOU CAN'T HELP FEELING INSPIRED AFTER HEARING THAT!
YES, THAT'S RIGHT!

I DON'T...
...HAVE A DREAM, MYSELF...

BLACK HAS A DREAM THAT HE'S REALLY ENTHUSI-ASTIC ABOUT.
CHEREN LOVES TO HELP OTHERS. YOU CAN ALWAYS COUNT ON HIM. AND I'VE COME TO DEPEND ON HIM...

DO YOU KNOW WHAT BROUGHT ME TO ANVILLE TOWN...?
NO... WHAT?

SOME-ONE IS *CHASING* ME...
WHO?! TEAM PLASMA?!

HE'S ***SO*** OVER-PROTECTIVE. HE DOESN'T WANT ME TO GO ON THIS JOURNEY.

HE'S DRAGGED ME HOME MORE TIMES THAN I CAN COUNT.

IT'S A BIG WORLD OUT THERE! YOU'RE TOO YOUNG TO HANDLE IT!!

I RUN AWAY...

...BUT HE KEEPS CATCHING ME. SO I RUN AWAY AGAIN...

MY DADDY!!

I HAVEN'T ACCOMPLISHED A ***THING*** ON THIS JOURNEY... EXCEPT RUNNING AWAY FROM HIM!

HE'S STILL SEARCHING FOR ME OUT THERE SOMEWHERE!

OH! AND I GOT ATTACKED BY TEAM PLASMA AND THEY TOOK MY POKÉMON TOO!!

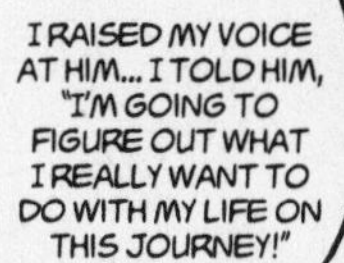

BUT... BUT... I HAVEN'T FIGURED OUT ***ANYTHING*** YET!

OHH... ***SNIFF***... WAAAH!

I HAVEN'T EVEN BEEN ABLE TO HELP OUT PROFESSOR JUNIPER... AND AFTER ALL THE SUPPORT SHE'S GIVEN ME...

YOU MUSTN'T GIVE UP...

...
BUT...
I DON'T
KNOW WHAT
TO DO
ANYMORE!

INGO!!
EMMET!!

YES...?
HOW
CAN I
BE OF
HELP
?!
I've
been
waiting
for you
to call
me!
tmp
tmp
tmp

WHICH TRAIN
GOES TO
CASTELIA CITY?
AND WHAT
TIME DOES IT
DEPART?!

CAS-
TELIA
CITY?
WHERE
ARE YOU
GOING?

CAFÉ...
...SONATA.

BIANCA! CAN YOU PLAY THAT TUNE AGAIN FOR ME?!
SURE.

CASTELIA CITY
NARROW STREET
HEY, WHERE ARE WE GOING? I DON'T LIKE THIS STREET.
I WAS LISTENING TO YOU PERFORM, AND I THOUGHT...

...YOU'RE NOT EXCEPTIONALLY GOOD AT PLAYING YOUR INSTRUMENT, BUT...

...THERE'S SOMETHING ABOUT YOUR PERFORMANCE THAT **TOUCHES THE HEART**.

OH, COME ON... YOU'RE JUST SAYING THAT TO CHEER ME UP!
NO, REALLY! I'VE BEEN WORKING IN SHOW BIZ FOR A LONG TIME. I CAN SENSE THESE THINGS...

YOU HAVE THAT CERTAIN SOMETHING... A MYSTERIOUS CHARM THAT TRANSCENDS TECHNIQUE AND LOOKS.
AND THAT'S WHAT I CONSIDER ***REAL TALENT***!

THE CAFÉ SONATA IS A FAMOUS CLUB. IT'S LAUNCHED A LOT OF FAMOUS MUSICIANS.
Café Sonata
THE GUITARIST HERE HEARD YOU PLAYING OVER THE XTRANSCEIVER AND HE'D LIKE YOU TO PLAY FOR HIM IN PERSON. THIS IS A GREAT OPPORTUNITY FOR YOU!
GOOD EVENING. IT'S ME, WHITE!

URGH ...
?!

WHITE...
BE CARE-FUL...
WHAT HAP-PENED HERE ...?!

AAH...!
WHITE!!
KRASH

A VULLABY !!

HOW ABOUT THAT?! I FINALLY, **FINALLY** MAN-AGED TO MEET A LEGENDARY POKÉMON...
A... LEG-ENDARY POKÉ-MON?

I'VE BEEN PLAYING MY GUITAR AT THIS CLUB ALL THIS TIME IN HOPES OF MEETING IT ONE DAY...
AND NOW I DID... BUT...

PCK
PCK
PCK
...**THAT** POKÉMON CAME CHASING AFTER IT!

SO... WHERE IS THE LEGEND-ARY POKÉ-MON?

HUH? A SONG ...?

THAT'S NOT A SONG! THAT'S ITS CRY!
RIGHT...
THE MELODY POKÉMON...
...MELOETTA.
I'VE HEARD THAT MANY MUSICIANS CREATED THEIR MASTERPIECES AFTER BEING INSPIRED BY ITS CRY.

DOROTHY!
PRO-
TECT
MELO-
ETTA!!
BOM
grab

kick

ZOOP
hide

IT'S SO FRIGHT-
ENED...

BUT...
BUT
I...
...CAN'T DO ANYTHING TO HELP!

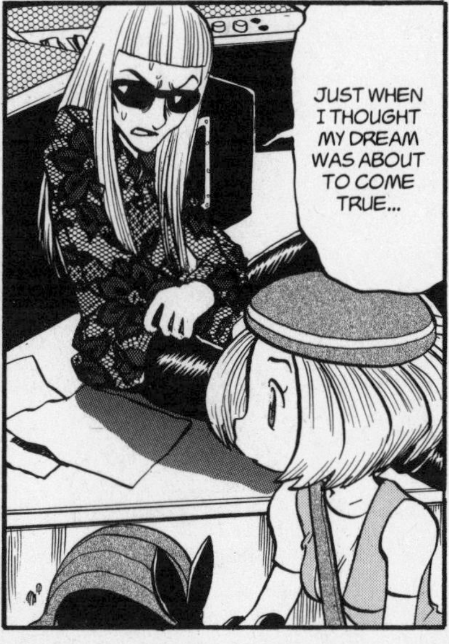
JUST WHEN I THOUGHT MY DREAM WAS ABOUT TO COME TRUE...

I HAD A TUNE I WANTED TO PLAY WITH MELOETTA... IF I EVER GOT TO MEET IT...
BUT... I CAN'T PLAY THE GUITAR WITH THIS ARM!

WHAT'S THE POINT ANY-
MORE ...?
WHAT HAVE I BEEN LIVING FOR UNTIL NOW ...?!

YOU MUSTN'T GIVE UP...

YOU...

...REALLY MUSTN'T GIVE UP.

More Adventures COMING SOON...

Helping a musician and a Pokémon in need helps Bianca finally discover her dream. And as Brycen rigorously trains Black, we learn about his dream before becoming a Gym Leader. Then flash back in time to see the beginning of Black's dream to become the Pokémon League Champion!

HOW DID BLACK CAPTURE HIS FIRST POKÉMON AND WHICH ONE WAS IT?

Plus, get to know Vullaby and Meloetta better and meet Stoutland, Unfezant and Rufflet!

VOL. 13 AVAILABLE DECEMBER 2013!

The Struggle for Time and Space Begins Again!

DVD VIDEO

Available at a DVD retailer near you!

Pokémon Trainer Ash and his Pikachu must find the Jewel of Life and stop Arceus from devastating all existence! The journey will be both dangerous and uncertain: even if Ash and his friends can set an old wrong right again, will there be time to return the Jewel of Life before Arceus destroys everything and everyone they've ever known?

Manga edition also available from VIZ Media

Pokémon
ARCEUS
AND THE
JEWEL OF LIFE

ratings.viz.com

www.viz.com

This way!

THIS IS THE END OF THIS GRAPHIC NOVEL!

To properly enjoy this VIZ Media graphic novel, please turn it around and begin reading from right to left.

This book has been printed in the original Japanese format in order to preserve the orientation of the original artwork. Have fun with it!

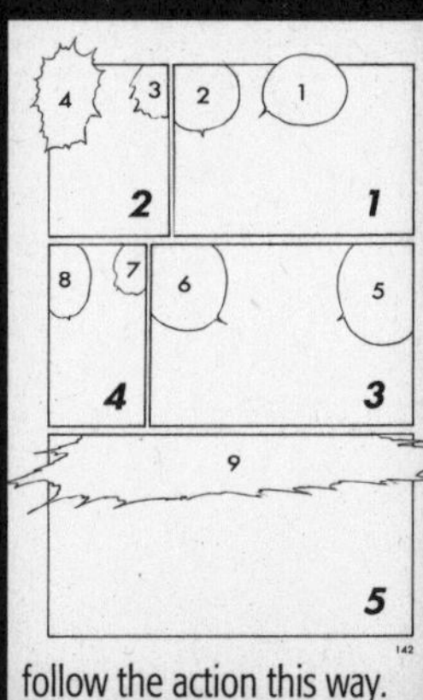

follow the action this way.